**For MacKenzie and Adyson,
our newest little monsters.**

Little, Brown and Company • Hachette Book Group • 237 Park Avenue, New York, NY 10017
Visit our website at www.lb-kids.com

Little, Brown and Company is a division of Hachette Book Group, Inc.
The Little, Brown name and logo are trademarks of Hachette Book Group, Inc.

First Edition: July 2011

Library of Congress Cataloging-in-Publication Data

Gall, Chris.
Substitute Creacher / Chris Gall. — 1st ed.
p. cm.
Summary: Mr. Creacher, a multi-tentacled substitute teacher, warns his prankish students not to misbehave, recounting rhyming cautionary tales of the weird, spooky, and unexpected.
ISBN 978-0-316-08915-9
[1. Stories in rhyme. 2. Behavior—Fiction. 3. Substitute teachers—Fiction. 4. Monsters—Fiction. 5. Schools—Fiction.]
I. Title.
PZ8.3.G1354Su 2011
[E]—dc22
2010019758

IM • Printed in China

10 9 8 7 6 5 4 3 2 1

Book design by Maria Mercado

The text was set in Mercurius and Bembo, and the display font is hand-lettered.
The artwork was created using bat wings, toad juice, and the bundled whiskers of a black cat.

SUBSTITUTE CREACHER

CHRIS GALL

LB
LITTLE, BROWN AND COMPANY
New York • Boston

O N A WINDSWEPT DAY in late October, the students of Ms. Jenkins's class arrived to a surprise at school.

"Substitute teacher today!" announced Peyton.

Amanda giggled and scribbled on the chalkboard. Luke performed a circus act. Gavin laughed like a mad scientist.

Then, at precisely eight o'clock, the door to the classroom creaked open. The substitute entered the room.

Amanda snickered at the way he spoke. Gavin opened a fresh box of tacks. The creature glared.

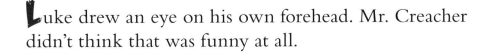

Luke drew an eye on his own forehead. Mr. Creacher
didn't think that was funny at all.

ATTENTION ALL SCAMPS, ALL RASCALS, AND FOOLS!

For forty-nine years
I've visited schools.
I've collected some tales
whose lessons are grave
about boys and girls
who didn't behave.
They'll give you the goose bumps.
They'll shiver your skin.
Now pay strict attention:
It's time we begin!

And with that, Mr. Creacher reached into his bag.

Then he pulled out a tattered file.

First we meet **KEITH**, a hungry young lad. Snacking on glue was a habit he had.

KEITH
CASE # 5B27

He ate so much glue— no amount was too much— that he started to stick to all he would touch!

Soon **NO ONE COULD FIND THE BOY UNDERNEATH** all of the objects that stuck to poor Keith.

Peyton's huge backpack fell over, and a dozen glue sticks rolled out. Mr. Creacher looked very unhappy.

Have you heard about SARA? She crammed all her stuff inside of her desk— but enough was enough!

SARA CASE #724C

Her desk was so full that it started to shake. It rattled and lurched like a minor earthquake.

Kids ran for their lives
and the teachers threw fits,
and then Sara's desk

BLEW ITSELF
INTO BITS!

Amanda passed a note to Luke, but Mr. Creacher snatched it from her hands.

KYLIE, the artist, was always the best at drawing when she should be taking a test.

When a dragon she drew looked so real it blew smoke, the children suspected it might be a joke.

But the dragon on paper then leapt from the page.

AUTHOR VISIT NEXT WEEK! BE READY
Dear Luke, I think you are cute
xo
Lunch Today TOTS -n- FRANKS
REPORT ALL STRANGE CREATURES
ARE YOU NOT YET CONVINCED?
Did I notice a yawn?
In case you're in doubt,
do let me go on!

Luke jumped when he felt a nibble inside his shirt pocket. Mr. Creacher opened another file.

KATE
CASE # 7299A

KATE always carried her backpack with pride. It made a great place for her monkey to hide!

CAFETERIA

Now, everyone knows the "NO PETS ALLOWED!" rule. When her monkey escaped, it wreaked havoc at school.

Then the children all thought they should bring a pet, too. Soon the school was a mess, **AND IT SMELLED LIKE A ZOO!**

Gavin quietly tied Amanda's shoelaces together.
Mr. Creacher scowled, then continued. . . .

HANK
CASE #114B1

Now, *this* impish fellow
(whose nickname was **HANK**),
like most little boys,
loved to pull a good prank.

He brought in a "guppy"
to enliven the class.
But in days it grew teeth
that could chomp
right through glass!

It wouldn't stop growing; its skin became dark. Now Hank really wished he'd not brought in a

SHARK!

Mr. Creacher paused and gazed upon the silent room.
Then he reached into his case one last time.

CHRIS
CASE #55923

And last we have **CHRIS**,
a mischievous sort,
with a fondness for thieving,
I'm sad to report.

It seems the poor boy
liked to trick for his treats:
Dressed like a monster,
he scared kids for sweets.

But then he stole candy
from a magical gnome.
Now the trick was on Chris.
He could **NEVER** go home. . . .

"Never?" Amanda gulped.
"Why?" whispered Peyton.

When he took off his costume,
Chris saw the gnome's curse.
He had seven green legs
and something much worse:
Dear Chris,
I'm sorry to
tell you this,
but
A note explained how,
for the rest of his days,
he'd teach other children
about wicked ways.

"Cool!" said Luke.

"I'm sorry, Mr. Creacher," said Amanda.

"You're the best substitute ever," said Gavin.

Mr. Creacher spied the clock on the wall.

It all happened here,
half a century ago,
at this very school.
I thought you should know.
Good-bye and good luck!
My time here is done.
I leave you a gift;
for each, there is one.

The students of Ms. Jenkins's class thanked Mr. Creacher for the candy and promised never to torment their teacher again. Then Mr. Creacher was gone.

*O*utside, Mr. Creacher looked in his case and saw that he had one last piece of the candy he had stolen so many years ago. He just needed someone to give it to. Then he noticed a small, old man nearby who wore a funny, familiar hat.

Mr. Creacher quietly slipped the candy into the man's pocket.

As the Substitute Creacher walked slowly down the windy street, he noticed a sweet smell in the autumn air. It was a smell he remembered from long ago.

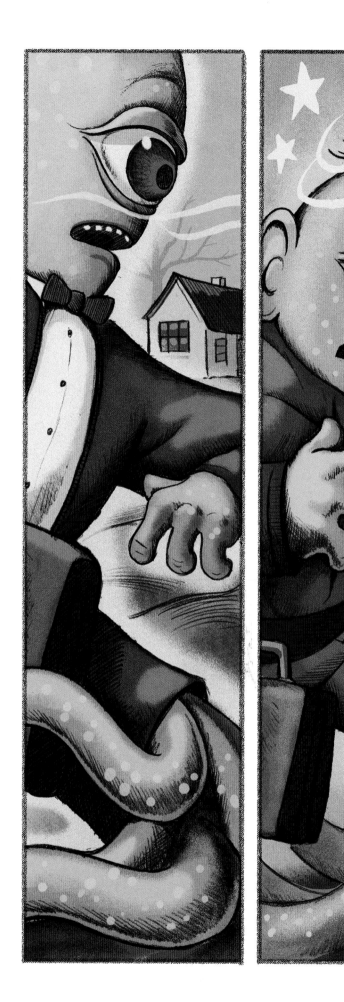

His tentacles tingled as the smell pulled him forward,
and the world started to spin around him. He began to run . . .

To a small house at the end of the street.

There, his bike was still leaning by the step, and his dog was still waiting on the lawn. Everything was as if he had never been gone. Chris was home.

And he was just in time for a Halloween treat.